MW01093517

For my children, at bedtime. - C.M.L.

For Leo - E.S.K

Text Copyright © Calee M. Lee 2017
Illustration Copyright © Erin Kenna 2017
All Rights Reserved.
No portion of this book may be reproduced
without express permission from the publisher.
ISBN:9781532401718 • eISBN: 9781532401848

Published in the United States
by Xist Publishing
www.xistpublishing.com

 xist Publishing

The Forest Sleeps

written by
Calee M. Lee

illustrated by
Erin Sunshine Kenna

The forest is a busy place at bedtime.

The deer amble into the thicket.

Sleep tight, deer.

The foxes curl up in
their dens.

Sleep tight, foxes.

The bears settle down in their cave.

Sleep tight, bears.

The rabbits dig into their burrow.

Sleep tight, rabbits.

The squirrel chatters
softly in his tree.

Sleep tight, squirrel.

The snake slinks under a log.
Sleep tight, snake.

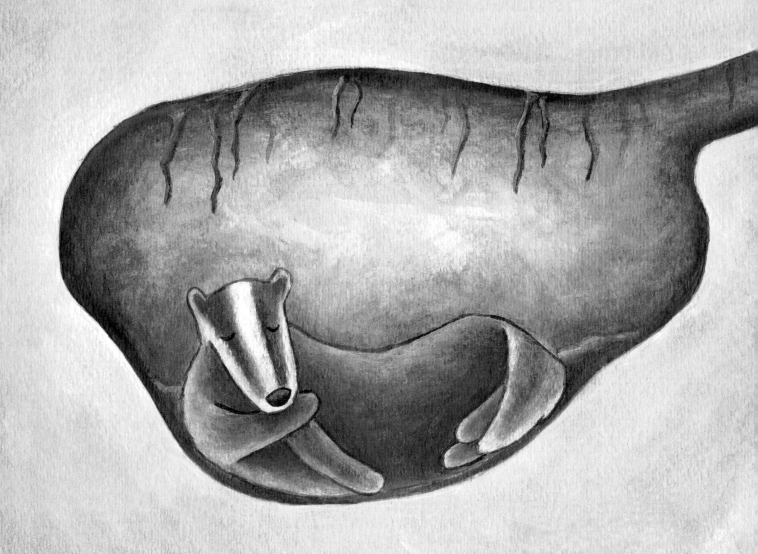

The badger tunnels into his sett.

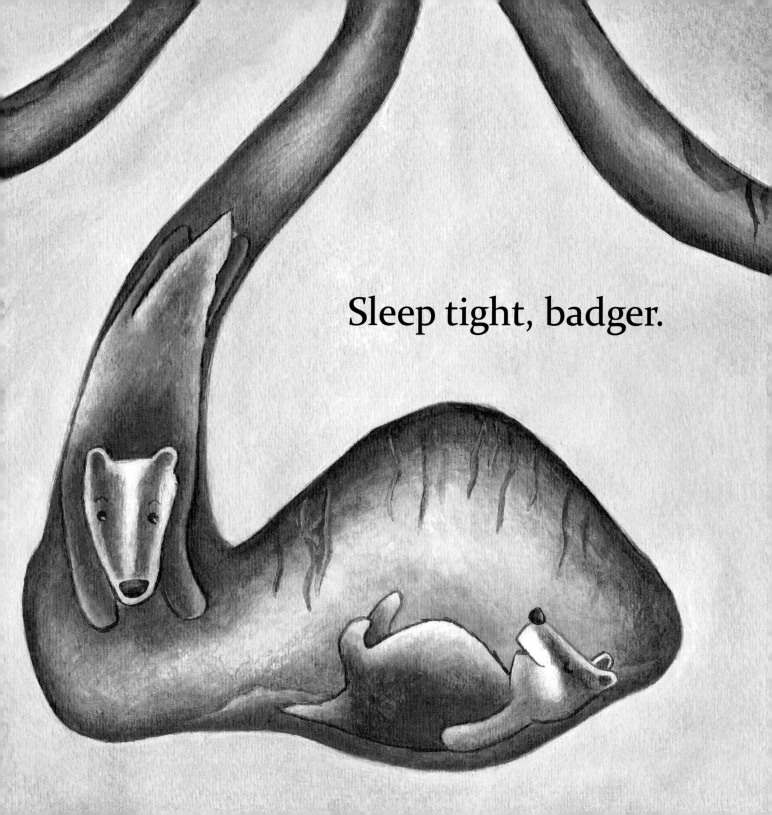

Sleep tight, badger.

The birds perch in their nest.

Sleep tight, birds.

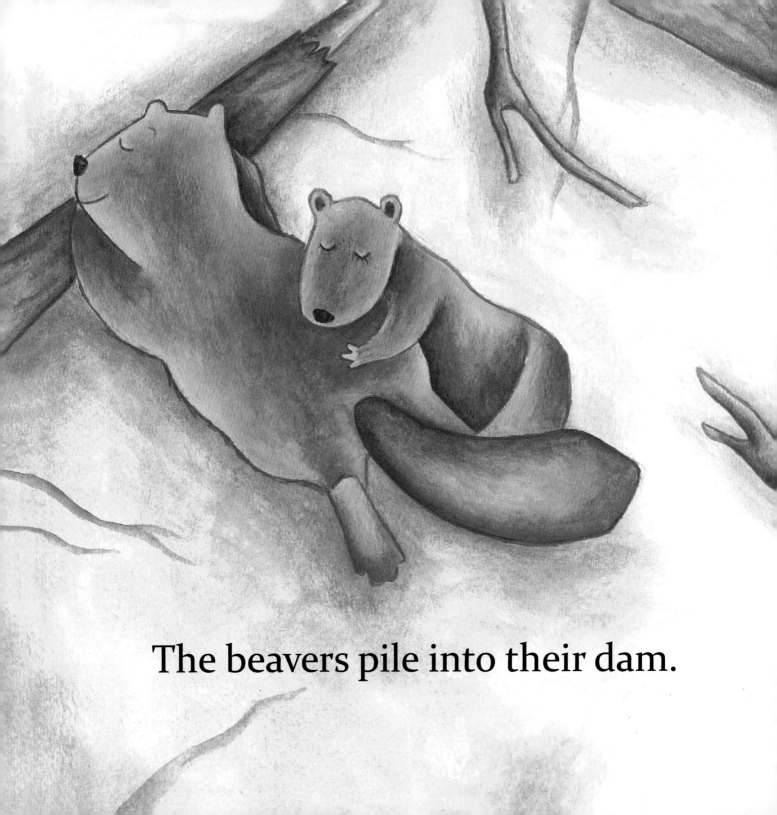

The beavers pile into their dam.

Sleep tight, beavers.

The fish rest in the reeds.

Sleep tight, fish.

The fireflies flit through the leaves.

Shine bright, fireflies.

The owls hoot
in the tree.

Keep watch, owls.

Sleep tight, forest.

71987811R00020

Made in the USA
Lexington, KY
26 November 2017